P9-DTR-196

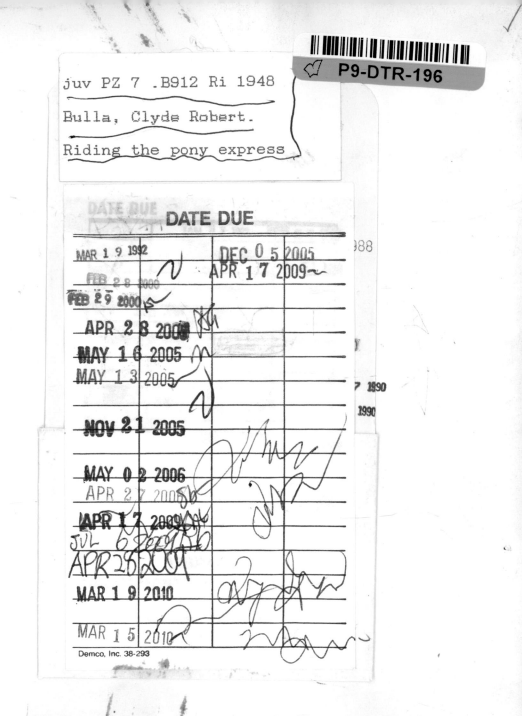

DATE DUE

Portia Lewis
PORTia
Lewiz
PORTIA
LEWIS

RIDING the PONY EXPRESS

RIDING the PONY EXPRESS

CLYDE ROBERT BULLA

Illustrated by Grace Paull

THOMAS Y. CROWELL COMPANY
NEW YORK

TO

Barbara Ann

Manufactured in the United States of America
Published in Canada by Fitzhenry & Whiteside Limited, Toronto

ISBN 0-690-70110-1   0-690-70111-X *(LB)*

17   18   19   20

CONTENTS

I

ST. JOE

It was late October in 1860, and the train moved slowly through the Missouri woods. Dick sat with his face close to the train window. As far away as he could see, there were hills and trees. There were a few houses, too. Most of them were made of logs, with rail fences in front of them.

He asked the man sitting next to him, "Are we nearly to St. Joe?"

"Yes," said the man. He looked hard at Dick. "Aren't you pretty young to be riding on the train by yourself?"

"I'll soon be eleven," said Dick.

"What is that tag around your neck?" asked the man.

"My Aunt Jane put it there." Dick tried to hide the tag under his coat. "She was afraid I might get lost."

"What does it say?" The man read the words on the tag:

> My name is Dick Park. I am on my way from New York to meet my father in St. Joseph, Missouri. Please help me get on the right trains.

"You didn't come all the way from New York by yourself!" said the man.

"Yes, I did," said Dick.

"Well, I never heard of such a thing!" said the man. "They tied a tag on you and sent you out here like a sack of corn!"

Dick didn't answer. He looked out the window again. Now he could see a town with smoke rising over the roofs.

"There it is—St. Joe!" said the man beside him.

All the people were picking up their bags and boxes. Dick picked up his carpetbag. It was nearly as big as he was.

The train stopped. There was a crowd in front of the station, and everyone was talking at once. Dogs were barking. There were horses and mules tied to the posts near the railroad track. Some of them stood quietly, but others snorted and rolled their eyes at the train.

As soon as Dick got off he was lost in the crowd. Soon he was standing with his back to the station. He looked up and down for his father.

Now the crowd was leaving. Only a few men were left. Dick looked at each one. His father was not there.

He went inside the station. There were bags setting along the wall. He put his carpetbag beside them. He spoke to the man behind the ticket-window. "Can you tell me where to find my father? His name is Tom Park."

The man was busy counting money. Without looking up, he shook his head.

Dick went outside again. He was tired from his long ride on the train. He wanted to wash his hands and face. Most of all, he wanted a drink of water and something to eat.

He walked down the street. He didn't know where to go or what to do. A cold wind was blowing across the river. Red and yellow leaves blew past him, and the air was full of dust.

Two men were coming toward him. They wore no feathers and had no bows and arrows, but Dick knew they were Indians by their dark faces and their long, black hair.

As they went by, they looked at the tag around his neck. Others looked at the tag, too. Aunt Jane had told him to wear it only as far as St. Joe. He pulled it off and threw it into the street. The wind carried it away. Dick was glad to see it go. He had not wanted to wear it in the first place.

Behind him someone began to shout, "Boy—boy!"

Dick looked back. A tall man with a black beard was coming down the street. He wore a big hat and he carried a pistol in his belt.

Dick walked faster. The man walked faster.

Dick started to cut across the street.

"Boy—stop!" called the man.

Dick started to run. Then he saw that a wagon and two horses were coming straight toward him.

"Whoa!" shouted the driver. He stood up in the wagon and pulled on the reins.

The horses were running so fast they couldn't stop. They were coming too fast for Dick to get out of the way. He was almost under the horses' feet, when a hand caught him from behind. Someone pulled him back. The wagon went by so close that it touched his coat.

Dick turned to see who had pulled him out of the way. It was the man with the black beard.

"See what you did!" said the man. "You nearly got run over!"

Dick couldn't say anything. He was out of breath.

"Why didn't you stop?" asked the man. "Did you think I was going to eat you alive?"

"What do you want with me?" asked Dick.

"I want to give you this. You dropped it just now." The man held out the tag Dick had worn around his neck.

"I didn't drop it. I threw it away," said Dick.

The man looked at the tag. "So your name is Dick Park. You aren't Tom Park's boy, are you?"

"Yes, I am," Dick said quickly. "Do you know my father?"

The man laughed, and Dick saw that behind the black beard his face was kind. "I guess I do know

your father. Maybe you've heard him talk about me. Sam Harper is my name."

"Sam Harper! Father wrote about you in every letter. He said you were one of his best friends." Dick held out his hand and the man shook hands with him.

"Your father and I used to hunt and trap together," Sam Harper told him. "He saved my life once. He pulled me out of the river when my boat turned over."

"And you saved my life just now," said Dick. "If it hadn't been for you, those horses would have run over me."

"Let's not talk about that now," said Sam Harper. "Let's go over to this eating house and I'll buy you your dinner."

"Thank you," said Dick, "but I have to find my father. Will you show me where he lives?"

"I could show you where he *used* to live."

"Doesn't he—doesn't he live here any more?"

"Come on over to the eating house," said Sam Harper, "and I'll tell you all about it."

1860   1861

II

THE PONY EXPRESS

They went into the eating house and sat down at a table. A girl brought them pork chops and potatoes. She brought baked beans and yellow cheese. She brought a glass of milk and a big dish of bread pudding for Dick.

"Are you hungry?" asked Sam.

"I'm not as hungry as I was," said Dick. "Where is my father? Why wasn't he here to meet me at the train?"

"Did he know you were coming?"

"My Aunt Jane sent him a letter. She sent it two weeks ago."

"If she sent it to St. Joe, he didn't get it," said Sam. "He left here a month ago. Your father is riding with the Pony Express."

"The Pony Express?"

"Don't you know what the Pony Express is?" asked Sam.

"Is it a train that carries the mail?"

"It carries the mail, but it isn't a train." Sam looked at the clock on the wall. "Finish your dinner, and I'll *show* you what the Pony Express is."

Dick finished his dinner. Sam led the way down the street. They stopped on a corner where a crowd was standing on the sidewalk.

Someone shouted, "Here comes the Pony Express!"

A horse and rider came in sight. They came down the street as fast as the wind. The horse was a black pony with a white star between his eyes. The rider was a young man in buckskin clothes and high

boots. The crowd gave a cheer. The man waved his hat as he went by.

On down the street he rode. For a little while Dick thought he was going to ride into the river. But a ferryboat was waiting at the end of the street. The rider rode out onto the boat.

The ferryboat took the horse and rider to the other side. The river was so wide that the man and the black horse looked very small, but Dick could see them as they left the boat. They went up a hill and into the woods along the river. Then they were gone.

"That was a Pony Express rider," said Sam. "He just crossed the Missouri River and now he is in Kansas. Did you see how he carries the mail?"

"No," said Dick.

"There's a piece of leather with a pocket in each corner," Sam told him. "It fits over the saddle, and the mail goes in the pockets. Most of the letters and papers go all the way to California."

"Why don't they go on the train?" asked Dick.

"The trains don't run any farther west than St. Joe. The Pony Express takes the mail from here. Those horses and riders keep on, day and night. They run into storms and mountains and bad Indians. But two days a week they start from St. Joe with that mail and two days a week they get to California."

"Doesn't it take a long time to get the mail to California?"

"Most of the time it gets there in ten days," said Sam. "Sometimes it takes only eight or nine days."

"Are you a Pony Express rider?" asked Dick.

"No. The Pony Express doesn't want big men. That makes too much for the horses to carry. Your father isn't a very big man, and he's one of the best riders in the country. That's why the Pony Express is glad to have him."

"But where is he? When is he coming back to St. Joe?"

"Maybe not for a long time. He went to ride in Nebraska."

"That's a long way off, isn't it?"

"Yes, a pretty long way," said Sam.

They walked up the street. The cold wind still blew across the river.

"I've got to go back to the station," said Dick. "I left my carpetbag there."

"Where are you going to stay tonight?"

"I don't know. Maybe I could sleep on a bench in the station."

"A bench would make a hard bed, and a cold one," said Sam. "Why don't you come home with me?"

IT TAKES A LOT OF TRAVELING

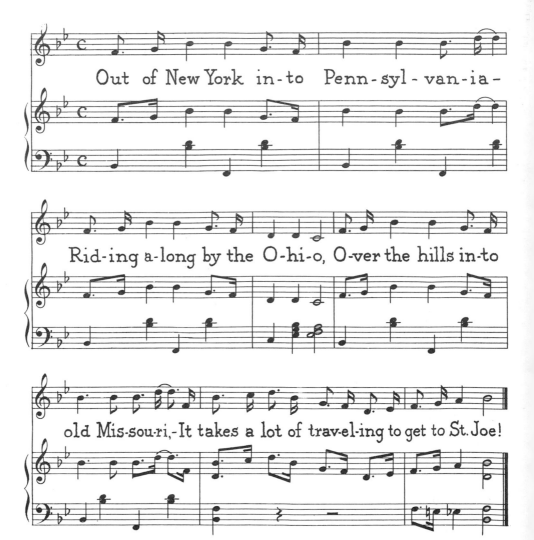

Out of New York in-to Penn-syl - van-ia-

Rid-ing a-long by the O-hi-o, O-ver the hills in-to

old Mis-sou-ri,-It takes a lot of trav-el-ing to get to St. Joe!

III

THE STAGECOACH

Sam carried Dick's carpetbag. They came to a stairway between two stores.

"I live up here," said Sam. "Your father used to live here, too."

Dick followed him up the stairs. Sam opened a door and led the way into a long, dark room. He struck a match on his boot and lit the lamp. "Pull up a chair," he said.

Dick pulled a chair up in front of the stove. There was not much in the room except the stove, two chairs, a bed, and a table.

Sam pointed to an animal skin on the wall. "That's a white wolfskin. You don't see many like that."

"Are you a trapper?" asked Dick.

"Yes," said Sam, "and in a few more days I'll start up the river to set my traps. But you can stay with me as long as I'm here."

"Thanks," said Dick, "but as soon as I can, I want to go where my father is."

"It takes a lot of traveling to get from New York to St. Joe. You'd better rest a while before you start on."

"I've got to go on," said Dick. "I don't have much money, and I haven't paid you yet for the dinner you bought me."

"Never mind about that. Why did they send you out here all by yourself?" asked Sam. "Why didn't your mother come with you?"

"I haven't any mother," said Dick. "I haven't anyone but Aunt Jane and Father, and Aunt Jane doesn't want me."

"Well, your father will want you," said Sam. "You can go up to Nebraska on the stage."

"The stage? Is that a stagecoach?"

"That's just what it is."

"When can I go?" asked Dick.

"A stage goes in the morning," said Sam.

"I want to go on that one."

"All right," said Sam, "if you can get up early enough."

Outside the wind was blowing harder. It was going to be a cold night.

Dick sat close to the fire. He was sleepy, and his eyes almost went shut. He was glad when Sam said it was time to go to bed.

But he wasn't glad to get up in the morning.

Sam shook the bed. He shook the pillow under Dick's head. "Time for breakfast! Time to get up!"

Dick shut his eyes tight. He tried to pull the covers over his face.

"Only an hour till the stage goes," said Sam.

As soon as Dick heard "stage," he opened his eyes. He jumped out of bed.

The room was full of smoke from the ham and eggs Sam was frying.

"Hurry and eat," said Sam. "While you were

asleep last night I went out and talked to the stage driver. There's a place for you on the stage this morning."

"How much money will it take?" asked Dick. "I haven't much left."

"That's all right," said Sam. "I paid the driver. Your father can pay me back sometime."

Dick ate his breakfast. He put on his coat.

"I can't find my cap," he said.

"That little cap won't keep you warm. I put it in your carpetbag," said Sam. "Here. I got you this one."

He gave Dick a brown fur cap.

Dick put it on. It came down over his ears, and the fur was soft and deep. "This is warm!" he said.

"Come on, now." Sam shut the door after them, and they went down the stairs.

It was early. Only a few people were on the street.

"There's the stage, in front of the hotel," said Sam.

The stagecoach was ready to go. Four horses were hitched to it.

There were two women and three men in the coach. They all spoke to Dick. One of the men said, "You can ride with me."

Dick got into the coach. He looked out the window and told Sam good-by.

"Good-by," said Sam. "I'll see you again sometime."

The driver shut the door. He climbed up on the high seat outside the coach. He cracked his whip, and they started off down the street.

IV

OWL CREEK STATION

The first two days out of St. Joseph were cold, but
the sun was bright. Part of the time Dick rode outside with the driver. While the coach rolled along,
the driver told him stories. He told him about Indians and hunters and the Pony Express.

"The coach carries mail, too. It carries the slow
mail," he said. "The Pony Express takes the fast
mail."

26

"Are we on the Pony Express trail now?" asked Dick.

"Yes," said the driver. "There are way stations all along this road. See that house with the log barn?"

"I see it," said Dick.

"That's a way station. The riders stop there to change horses. They change horses every ten or fifteen miles."

Dick heard the sound of a horse's hoofs. A horse and rider came around the bend. The rider had a red handkerchief around his neck.

"It's a Pony Express rider!" said Dick. "I can see the mail pockets on his saddle."

"Hello!" called the driver. "Is everything all right?"

"All's well along the road!" the rider called back, and he was gone.

"He was taking the California mail back to St. Joe," said the driver. "The mail has to go both ways. Before we get to Nebraska, you may see more of the Pony Express."

While the sun was shining, Dick liked to ride on the high seat with the driver. But after a few days he was glad to stay inside the coach. The sky was dark, and rain fell. The road turned to mud.

Every night they slept at one of the coach stations along the road. Every morning when Dick got up he hoped the sky would be clear. But it kept on raining.

They came to the prairies of Nebraska. The land was flat and bare.

The driver told Dick one morning, "We'll get to your father's station today."

Dick kept his face close to the window. He saw a sign, "Owl Creek Station." Then he saw a log cabin with smoke coming out of the chimney.

The coach stopped.

"Here you are." The driver handed Dick's carpetbag down off the top of the coach. He cracked his whip and waved good-by.

Dick ran through the rain to the cabin. He knocked on the door.

A woman opened the door. "Oh!" she cried. "What do you want?"

"I want to come in," said Dick.

"Well, come in, then. Now," she said, when he had shut the door, "who are you? Where did you come from?"

A man came out of the next room. His mouth fell open.

"Father!" said Dick.

"Dick!" said the man. "I can't believe it! Dick, how did you get here?"

"I came on the stagecoach."

"But Son, why didn't you let me know?"

"Aunt Jane sent you a letter. She sent it to St. Joe, and you weren't there."

"You didn't come from New York by yourself?"

"Yes, I did."

All at once, Tom Park's face was angry. "What did Aunt Jane mean by sending you out here all alone?"

"She said it was time I came out West to live with you."

Mr. Park looked at Dick, then at the woman, who was still in the room. "I ride for the Pony Express," he said. "You know that, don't you, Son? I don't have a real home. I don't know whether I can keep you here at the way station or not."

A shout went up outside.

"I've got to go. The mail has to be on time." Mr. Park said to the woman, "Mrs. Kelly, this is my son. Take care of him for me. Dick, we'll have a long talk when I get back." He threw on his raincoat and ran out the door.

"Come quick!" said the woman. "You can see them change the Pony Express mail."

Dick went to the window. Out in the road were two horses. One looked tired and its legs were muddy. The other was shaking its head and kicking up its heels.

"Look," said the woman. "George Gates just got here with the mail. See them putting the mail on the other horse? It never takes them over two minutes to change. There goes your father up in the saddle. Look at him ride!

"Now," said the woman, "here comes George Gates to the house. He has had a long, hard ride. George will stay here until your father comes back with more mail."

"When will my father come back?" asked Dick.

"Not for three days." Mrs. Kelly looked out the window again. "There goes my husband, taking George's horse to the stable. In all this rain, too. I'll go make him a pot of good, hot coffee."

Dick looked out into the rain. Aunt Jane had sent him all the way from New York because she didn't want him. Now it looked as if his father didn't want him, either.

V

THE KELLY FAMILY

George Gates came in. He was a thin young man with freckles on his nose. He took off his wet coat.

"I'll fix you a bite to eat," said Mrs. Kelly.

"No," said George. "I rode nearly all night and half of today. All I want to do now is rest."

"Go to the bedroom, then," said Mrs. Kelly. "You can eat when you get up."

George went into the bedroom. Mrs. Kelly went into the kitchen. Dick was left alone.

He walked about the big room. In one end was a ladder that led to a <u>loft</u>. In the other end was a fireplace.

On a shelf above the fireplace were arrows and Indian dishes. There was a fur rug in front of the fire. Dick put his hand on it. Then he jumped. Someone had come up behind him.

It was a girl. She was almost as tall as he was. She had black hair and blue eyes.

"Hello," she said.

"Hello," said Dick.

"Are you going to stay here?"

"I don't know."

"I live here. I'm Katy Kelly."

Dick sat down in a chair by the fireplace.

"I know your name," the girl said. "Mama told me." She sat down on the rug. "Do you see this fur? It came from a <u>grizzly</u> bear. My father killed it. He used to hunt all the time till he fell off a horse and hurt his leg."

Dick said nothing.

"Why don't you talk to me?" asked Katy.

"I don't want to talk," said Dick.

Katy went away. In a little while she was back. "Come and get something to eat," she said.

Dick went to the kitchen. There was a big dish of stew on the table. There were corn cakes and molasses, and Mrs. Kelly had made tea.

The back door opened and Mr. Kelly came in. He had black hair and blue eyes like Katy's. He was lame, and he walked as if his leg hurt him.

"Are you Tom Park's boy?" he asked.

"Yes, sir," said Dick.

"I hope you grow up to be as fine a man as your father," said Mr. Kelly. "Sit down, all of you. This dinner looks good."

Dick drank his tea. He ate a corn cake. His dish of stew was thick and salty, and he couldn't eat it all.

"Are you sick?" asked Mr. Kelly.

"No, sir," said Dick.

"Eat your stew, then," said Mr. Kelly.

"I don't want it."

"Out here we don't throw anything away," Mr. Kelly told him. "Eat your stew, boy."

Dick put down his spoon. He got up from the table and walked out of the room.

He stood by the fireplace. Mrs. Kelly came out of the kitchen.

"Did I give you too much stew?" she asked.

Dick nodded.

"Next time I won't give you so much. Mr. Kelly doesn't mean to be cross. But sometimes his leg hurts him and he says cross things." She went to the ladder that led to the loft. "Do you want to see where you are going to sleep?"

Dick climbed the ladder after her. There were potatoes on the floor of the loft. There were onions hanging on the wall.

"I'll have to make you a bed on the floor," said Mrs. Kelly, "but it will be soft."

It *was* a soft bed. It was a featherbed. When Dick lay down that night and pulled the buffalo robe over him, he found it was a warm bed, too. But out on the prairie the wolves and coyotes were howling, and it was a long time before he could go to sleep.

COME ON, LITTLE PONY

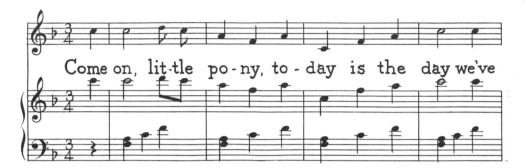

Come on, lit-tle po-ny, to-day is the day we've

got to start hit-ting the trail. — Come on, lit-tle po-ny, lets

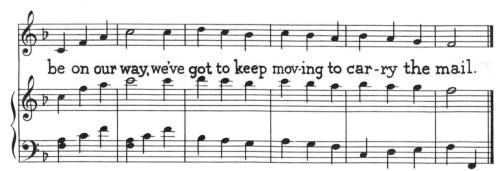

be on our way, we've got to keep mov-ing to car-ry the mail.

VI

THE STABLE

Two days went by. The morning came when Dick
woke up and saw his father climbing into the loft.

"Hello, Son!" said Mr. Park.

"Father!" Dick sat up in bed. "When did you
get back?"

"I carried the mail in last night and George Gates
was waiting to take it on. I got up early so I could
talk to you." Mr. Park sat down on a box by the bed.
"I talked to Mr. Kelly about you last night."

"What did he say?" asked Dick.

"He says you can stay. The Kellys haven't much room here, and I didn't know whether they would keep you or not. But it's all right. Mr. Kelly needs a boy to help him with the cow and the horses."

"I don't want to stay here," said Dick.

Mr. Park looked surprised. "Why not?"

"Mr. Kelly doesn't like me. And I don't like the prairie. It's flat and ugly and cold, and the wolves and coyotes <u>howl</u> at night."

"It isn't bad when you get used to it."

"I don't want to get used to it. I don't want to stay."

Mr. Park said, "Now that you're here, there's nothing else for you to do."

Dick looked at his father. "Do you remember what you told me before you came out West?"

"Yes, I remember. I said I was going to make a home for us, where we could be together all the time. We *are* going to have a home some day. But now I have my work here. That comes first."

"Why does it come first?" asked Dick.

"Our country is in trouble," said Mr. Park. "Soon the North and South may be at war. I think of our Pony Express as a chain to hold the East and West together. Every little way station, every rider, everyone who helps is part of the chain. Don't you want to be part of it, too?"

"Not if I have to stay here," said Dick.

Mr. Park stood up. "Sometimes we all have to do things we don't want to do. You're old enough to know that. Put on your clothes and come down."

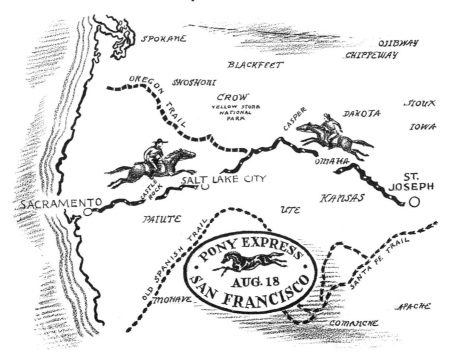

Later that morning Dick and his father walked down the road to the stable. There were six horses in the <u>stalls.</u> Two were Mr. Kelly's. The other four were Pony Express horses.

Mr. Park told Dick the names of the Pony Express horses. The two black ones were Prince and Dandy. The spotted pony was Bonnie.

They came to the pony in the last stall. "This is Lady," said Mr. Park.

Lady nodded her head as if she were saying, "How do you do?" Her eyes were soft and gentle. Her coat was white.

"The horses have to be fed and watered," said Mr. Park. "Mr. Kelly will tell you how to take care of them. You know how to ride, don't you?"

"A little," said Dick.

"Mr. Kelly may let you ride some of the horses. I want you to have some good times here."

Dick didn't answer. He could see no good times ahead as long as he stayed here. He could see nothing but work at the stable, with the bare, cold prairie on all sides of him.

VII

WORK AT THE STABLE

While Mr. Park was at the station, he showed Dick how to brush the horses and comb their manes and tails. He showed him how to <u>saddle</u> and <u>bridle</u> a horse. He told him how to clean the stable and fill the feed boxes and carry water from the well.

One morning they walked together out across the prairie. The rain was over, but the grass was still wet.

Mr. Park picked up something at his feet. It was an Indian arrowhead. He gave it to Dick.

"This is a good place to find arrowheads," said Mr. Park. "The Indians had a battle here a long time ago."

"Are there any Indians here now?" asked Dick.

"Yes," said his father. "Most of them are our friends. But farther west the Indians are not so friendly. Some of them would scalp any Pony Express rider they caught."

"Do they ever catch the Pony Express riders?"

"They try, but they don't often catch one. Our men are good riders."

"Aren't the Indians good riders, too?"

"Yes, but our horses are better and faster. We take good care of our horses. An Indian lets his horse take care of himself."

Mr. Park stopped. "Look."

A little brown animal had just come out of a hole in the ground. It sat up on its hind legs and held out its paws.

Mr. Park laughed. "It looks like a dog begging for a bone. Listen to it bark and scold. That's a prairie dog. You'll see lots of them here. They make trouble for the Pony Express."

"How could they make trouble?"

"They dig holes in the ground. If a horse gets a foot into one of them, it might throw the rider. It might break the horse's leg, too."

Mr. Park pointed. "The river is that way. Some day we'll go over there. But now we'd better go back to the station. George Gates will be here with the mail today."

George Gates rode up to the station that afternoon. Mr. Park was waiting with a fresh horse. He rode away with the mail.

Mr. Kelly called Dick. "Come and take George's horse to the stable."

Dick led the horse to the stable. He went to the house.

Mr. Kelly was in the doorway. "Did you feed and water the horses?"

"No, sir," said Dick.

"Go do it," said Mr. Kelly. "Everybody has to work here."

Dick went back to the stable. He thought of running away. But he had nowhere to go. Only out across the prairie. He would soon be lost there.

There was a sound behind him. Lady was stamping her feet in her stall.

Dick patted her neck. "Hello, Lady," he said.

He knew the horses were not to blame because he didn't like it here. They couldn't help it because he had to stay.

He filled the feed boxes with corn and threw hay into the mangers. He stopped in front of Lady's stall.

"There," he said. "Is that what you wanted?"

Lady put her head over the manger and rubbed her nose softly against him.

INDIAN BOY

Ind-ian boy, Ind-ian boy, who has seen an

Ind-ian boy With a feath-er in his hair,

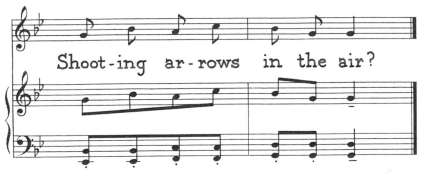

Shoot-ing ar-rows in the air?

VIII

THE INDIAN BOY

There was no school for Dick and Katy to go to, so Mrs. Kelly had school for them at home. Every morning they had lessons in reading, writing, spelling, and numbers.

One day after their lessons Mrs. Kelly said, "It isn't very cold today. Would you like to take two of the horses and go for a little ride?"

"Oh, yes!" Katy jumped up and down. "Did Father say we could go?"

"Yes," said Mrs. Kelly. "He says it isn't good for the horses to stand so long in the stable."

Katy and Dick ran out of the house.

"I'm going to ride Bonnie," said Katy.

"I'll ride Lady," said Dick.

"I'm not going to put a saddle on Bonnie. I'm going to ride like an Indian." Katy climbed up on the spotted pony's back. "You can't ride like this. You'd fall off."

"I would not." Dick climbed up on Lady's back. They rode away.

Katy stood up on the spotted pony's back. Her hair blew out behind her. "You can't do this."

"I can, too." Dick stood up on Lady's back. It was hard for him to do, but he rode a little way before he sat down again.

"You don't like the prairie, do you?" said Katy.

"No, I don't."

"It's pretty in the spring when the grass is green. It's pretty by the river, too, with the willow trees and

cottonwoods and cattails. You've never been to the
river, have you?"

"No," said Dick.

"Let's ride over there," said Katy. "It isn't far."

They rode to the river. There were rocks and
deep ditches along the banks.

"Look at the paths down the sides of the ditches,"
said Dick. "What made them?"

"I don't know," said Katy. "They may be buffalo paths."

"Here's a wide one. It's wide enough for the
horses." Dick started to ride down it. Katy rode
behind him.

"It's getting steep," she said.

"Let's go back." Dick started to turn Lady
around. Just then an arrow sailed over his head and
hit the bank beside Katy.

"Oh, oh!" she cried.

Someone looked up over the rocks ahead. It was
an Indian boy. He wore a feather in his hair and his
face was red with paint. He carried a bow and he
had two arrows in his belt.

When he saw Dick, he turned and ran.

"Here. Hold Lady." Dick threw the reins to Katy and slid off his horse. He started after the Indian boy.

Down over the rocks they ran. The Indian boy came to the bottom of the ditch. He went climbing up the other side like a squirrel. But halfway up the bank he dropped his bow. He stopped and tried to pick it up.

Dick was close behind him. He jumped and caught the Indian boy by the leg.

"Come back here!" He pulled the Indian boy back down the bank. "You nearly hit us with that arrow. What did you do that for?"

The Indian boy looked scared. "Me no shoot at you! Me shoot at rabbit!"

"And you didn't want to hurt us?" asked Dick.

"No, no! Me friend."

"If you're a friend, what did you run for?"

"White boy look mad."

"White boy *was* mad," said Dick. "I thought you were trying to shoot us."

"No, no," the Indian boy said over and over.

"I'll let you go," said Dick. "After this, you look where you shoot."

"Oh, yes. Me look good." The Indian boy started up the bank. He climbed out of sight.

Dick went back to Katy and the horses.

"The Indian boy didn't want to hurt us. He was shooting at a rabbit."

"No, he wouldn't try to shoot us," said Katy. "That was Little Bear."

"Do you know him?" asked Dick.

"Yes. He lives on old Billy Black's ranch up the river. His father works there." Katy began to laugh. "He looked funny when he stuck his head up over the rocks."

"Why does he wear that red paint on his face?" asked Dick.

"He was just playing. He wanted to look like a big Indian."

"I don't think he is a bad boy," said Dick.

"No, but the men on the Black ranch are bad. My father says so," Katy said, as they rode toward home. "My father thinks they take people's horses."

"Why doesn't someone stop them?"

"If they come around our house," said Katy, "someone *will* stop them."

THE PRETTY GIRL DRESSED IN BLUE

See the pret-ty girl dressed in blue, See the rib-bons a-

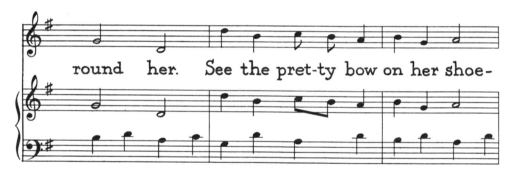

round her. See the pret-ty bow on her shoe-

Aren't you glad you found her?

IX

CHRISTMAS AT THE STATION

Snow came to the prairie. Katy was glad. "We're going to have a white Christmas!" she said.

Dick wished he could give presents to everyone at the station, but he had nothing to give. He remembered that he had seen a little pine tree by the river. A few days before Christmas he rode over and brought the tree back to the station.

"A Christmas tree!" cried Katy. "Dick has brought me a Christmas tree!"

"It's a present for us all," said Mrs. Kelly.

They set the tree in front of the fireplace. Katy made strings of red, yellow, and blue corn to put on its branches. She made paper chains, too, and a star for the top.

"It's the best Christmas tree I ever had," she said.

The day before Christmas, Dick's father rode up with the mail. Dick took his horse to the stable. When he went back to the house, his father was getting warm by the fire.

"Did the snow cover all the trail?" asked Mr. Kelly.

"Yes, it did," said Mr. Park. "There was just one way I could find the road. I looked for the weeds sticking up through the snow on each side."

"Your horse was tired," said Dick.

"I know. I had to ride hard to get here on time." Mr. Park took off his boots. "But we change horses every ten or fifteen miles. The men have to keep going for seventy-five miles or more before resting."

Katy came running in. "See our Christmas tree? Dick found it."

"It's a fine one," said Mr. Park. "It's the first one I've seen this winter."

"Are you going to sit up with us on Christmas Eve?" asked Katy.

"No, I'm going to bed now," said Mr. Park, "but I'll be up all day on Christmas."

On Christmas day Dick sat by the fire with his father and Mr. Kelly. Katy and her mother were busy in the kitchen. Katy had on her best blue dress and a long, white apron. Every little while she ran in for another look at the tree.

"Wait till you see what we have for dinner," she would say, "and don't you peep, either!"

Outside they heard the sound of wheels on the snow.

"It's the stage," said Mr. Park.

"And it's stopping." Mr. Kelly went to the door.

The driver had jumped down off the stagecoach and was carrying a box up to the house. "Merry Christmas. Here is something for Dick Park," he said, and was gone again.

Katy and her mother came out of the kitchen.

"What is it?—what is it?" cried Katy. "Dick, why don't you open it?"

Dick sat down and opened the box. He took out a piece of paper. "Father, look! It says, 'Merry Christmas, from your friend Sam Harper'!"

There were two presents in the box. One was a hunting knife with a long, sharp blade. The other was a white wolfskin. "It is the same wolfskin I saw in his room in St. Joe," said Dick. "This is a surprise. I wasn't looking for presents, and now I have two."

"Then I have another surprise for you." His father went into the bedroom and brought out another box. "Merry Christmas, Son."

Dick opened the box. "Look, Katy!" he shouted. "Look, everybody!"

It was a pair of boots just like his father's, only much smaller.

"Thank you, Father." He put on the boots. He put the knife in his belt and threw the wolfskin over his shoulder. "Now I look like a real hunter."

There were presents for Katy, too. There were three hair ribbons and a doll with a yellow dress. She liked them so much she kept them by her plate while she ate dinner.

And what a dinner it was! There were apples in the middle of the table. There were rabbits and baked potatoes, milk and coffee, biscuits and butter, apple jelly, white cake, and pumpkin pie.

"Katy made the biscuits," said Mrs. Kelly.

"Katy is a good cook," said Mr. Park. "These biscuits are as light as a feather."

"What are we going to do with so much food?" asked Mr. Kelly.

"If there is any left we can have it for supper."

But there was very little left for supper.

After dinner they sat around the Christmas tree. The men told stories. Katy brought out a guitar. "Play and sing for us, Father," she said.

Mr. Kelly laughed and took the guitar. "This is your song, Katy," he said. He played and sang a song about a pretty girl dressed in blue.

Dick was surprised. He had never heard Katy's father laugh and play and sing before.

Mr. Kelly played some more, and they all sang. Then Mrs. Kelly brought some apples to eat by the fire.

Before Dick knew it, the day was gone.

"I'm going to sleep in the loft with you," said his father.

They climbed the ladder and went to bed. Mr. Park blew out the candle.

"This has been a good Christmas, hasn't it, Son?"

"Yes," said Dick. He wished every day could be Christmas and that his father could be with him all the time.

X

LITTLE BEAR COMES TO DINNER

After Christmas there were days of rain and the snow melted. The ice broke up on the river. One morning the sun came out through the clouds.

"Turn the cow out in the sun," said Mr. Kelly.

"Shall I tie her up?" asked Dick.

"No," said Mr. Kelly. "She won't go far."

Dick turned the cow out.

"Come to the house, Dick," called Mrs. Kelly. "It's time for your lessons."

He and Katy had their lessons. Then Mr. Kelly told Dick, "Take the cow back to the stable. It's getting cold fast. There may be a storm."

Dick went outside. The cow was gone. He took one of the horses and went to look for her. He rode as far as the river. He looked in some of the ditches, but the cow was not there.

All at once he heard a cry. Something was moving near the water.

Dick jumped off his horse. He ran down the steep bank. There on the sand lay Little Bear, the Indian boy. His hair and clothes were wet.

"Little Bear!" said Dick. "Are you hurt?"

"No. Me cold." When the Indian boy tried to get up, he fell over on the sand. "Me fall in water. Now legs no work. Feet no work."

Dick saw that Little Bear was so cold his legs would not hold him up. The water was turning to ice on his clothes.

"You've got to get up. You'll freeze if you

don't." Dick helped him to his feet. He worked the
Indian boy's arms up and down. He rubbed his legs.

"Can you walk now?" he asked.

Little Bear took a step. He took another. Dick
helped him. It was a long, slow climb up the bank.
When they got to the top, Little Bear wanted to stop
and rest.

"No," said Dick. "It's getting colder all the time. I'm going to take you to a warm place."

Dick helped the Indian boy up on the horse and got on behind him. They rode back to the station as fast as the horse could go.

Katy came to the door. "Oh, Dick, we found the cow! She was in the trees by the creek . . ." Katy stopped. She was looking at Little Bear.

"He was in the river," said Dick. "We've got to get him dry and warm."

Mrs. Kelly brought a blanket and they put Little Bear in it. They hung most of his clothes by the fire.

Mr. Kelly came in. "What's that Indian doing here?"

"He was in the river," Dick said. "I brought him here."

"Well, get him out as soon as you can. I don't want anyone from Billy Black's ranch in my house." Mr. Kelly went into the kitchen.

Little Bear moved his head. He moved his fingers and toes.

"Me warm now," he said.

He stood up. He walked across the room.

"Me go home."

Dick smelled the stew cooking for dinner. He said, "I wish I could give him something to eat before he goes."

"He does look hungry," said Mrs. Kelly.

Dick went to the kitchen. He put some stew into a dish. Mr. Kelly was watching. "What are you going to do with that?"

"I'm going to take it to Little Bear," said Dick.

"There won't be enough to feed you and Little Bear, too," said Mr. Kelly. "If you give him that, you'll go without your dinner."

Dick said nothing. He took the dish to the Indian boy.

Little Bear's eyes grew bright when he saw the stew. First he ate all the potatoes, onions, and buffalo meat. Then he drank what was left.

"Me go now," he said.

Dick watched him go. "I hope he gets home all right."

"He will," said Katy. "Indians are strong."

Mrs. Kelly called Dick and Katy to dinner.

"I can't have any dinner," said Dick.

"Why not?" asked Katy.

"I gave mine to Little Bear." Dick put on his coat and cap and went to the stable. He gave the horses some corn. He sat down on the hay.

After a while Katy came into the stable. "Father didn't mean to be cross. His leg hurts him today," she said. "Here, I brought you some of my dinner." From under her apron she took a biscuit, a piece of buffalo meat, and two cookies.

"Thanks," said Dick. "You eat one of the cookies."

"No. They are for you." Katy sat by him until he was through eating. "You'd better come to the house," she told him.

They went into the kitchen. Mr. Kelly was sitting at the table.

"Dick," he asked, "are you hungry?"

"No, sir," said Dick.

"You must be hungry. There was enough for you and the Indian boy, after all." Mr. Kelly said to his wife, "Bring Dick something to eat."

Mrs. Kelly brought a bowl of stew. She brought bread and butter and milk and cookies. And so Dick had two dinners instead of none.

XI

ALONE AT THE STATION

"The days are getting longer," George Gates said to Dick one morning. "Spring will soon be here."

They were sitting on the sunny side of the cabin. George had been showing Dick how to shoot his pistol.

"I'll be glad when spring comes," said Dick.

"So will I. This was a bad winter for the Pony

Express. Sometimes the snow in the mountains was too deep for the horses."

"What did the riders do?"

"They took the mail on foot. I could tell you a lot of stories about riders who had to carry the mail on foot."

Mrs. Kelly was in the doorway. "Before you start telling stories, come on to dinner," she said.

In the kitchen, they all sat down at the table.

"Where is the fish?" asked Mr. Kelly.

"What fish?" asked Mrs. Kelly.

"There was fish left over from yesterday."

"There were just two pieces," said Mrs. Kelly. "I'm going to throw them out."

"Don't throw good food away," said Mr. Kelly.

"But the fish may not be good now," said Mrs. Kelly.

Mr. Kelly went to the cupboard. He found the plate of fish. "This looks good. Who wants some?"

"I don't," said Mrs. Kelly.

"This jack rabbit is good enough for me," said George.

"Me, too," said Dick.

"Then Katy and I will eat the fish, won't we, Katy?" Mr. Kelly took one piece of fish and put the other on Katy's plate.

Katy ate only half of hers. "I'm not very hungry," she said.

"I'm hungry all the time," said George. "When I ride with the mail I think about what I'll have to eat at the next station."

"Will you be riding again tonight?" asked Dick.

"Yes, as soon as your father gets here with the mail." George got up from the table. "I'm going to bed now. I want to get all the sleep I can before I start out tonight."

After dinner Dick and Katy played tag.

"Be quiet, children," said Mrs. Kelly. "George wants to sleep. Why don't you read your books?"

Katy picked up a book and put it down again. "I don't feel good," she said.

"Why, Katy! Your face is so white," said Mrs. Kelly. "Where do you feel sick?"

"All over," said Katy.

Mr. Kelly came out of the kitchen and fell into a chair. "I feel sick," he said.

Katy was crying. "I'm so sick!"

"I know what's the matter. That fish you ate for dinner was not good." Mrs. Kelly ran to the bedroom. "George! George Gates, get up!"

George rubbed his eyes. "What do you want?"

"Katy and her father are sick. They need a doctor."

"George, get up quick," said Mr. Kelly. "Take us to town to the doctor."

George got up. "Can't I ride to town and tell the doctor to come out?"

"No, no! That would take too long," said Mr. Kelly.

George and Dick ran to the stable. Dick led Mr. Kelly's two horses outside. George hitched them to the wagon.

He drove up in front of the house. He helped Katy and Mr. Kelly into the wagon.

"Can you drive them to town, Mrs. Kelly?" asked George.

"No," said Mrs. Kelly. "The horses are too wild for me to drive. They are too wild for Dick to drive, too. You'll have to go, George."

"But it's a long way to town. I wouldn't be back in time to meet Dick's father and carry the mail tonight."

"Don't stand there and talk!" cried Mr. Kelly. "We've got to get to the doctor!"

"Listen, Dick," said George, "when your father comes tonight, tell him what happened. Tell him to carry the mail on to the next station. All right?"

"Yes," said Dick.

Katy lay in the wagon. "Mama—I want mama!" she cried.

"I've got to go along," said Mrs. Kelly. "I can hold her on the way to town." She got into the wagon. "You won't be afraid, Dick?"

"No," he said.

The wagon started down the road. Dick watched until it was out of sight.

He took his reading book and went to the stable. He sat on the hay and read his lesson out loud to the horses. Lady nodded her head as if she understood every word.

It was nearly dark when he heard a sound outside the stable. The door opened and a brown face looked in. It was the Indian boy.

"Little Bear!" said Dick. "I'm glad you came. I'm here all alone."

"Me know."

"How did you know?"

"Me hear men talk at ranch. They see wagon

go by. They know you alone. Tonight they come."

"The men from the ranch are coming here?" asked Dick.

"Yes."

"What for?"

"They want horses," said Little Bear. "You hide. They bad. They hurt you."

He shut the door. When Dick looked out, the Indian boy was gone.

XII

THE FIRE

Dick tried to think what to do. There were no neighbors he could go to for help. He could not fight the men from the Black ranch. But he knew he was not going to let them take Lady or any of the other horses.

He waited until it was dark. Then he tied three of the horses together, one behind the other. He tied the cow behind the horses. He rode Lady and led them all off across the prairie to the river.

He found a place where willow trees grew by the river bank. He tied the horses and cow to the trees. The men from the Black ranch would never find them here.

Dick walked up and down to keep warm. He talked to the horses to let them know he had not left.

After a while he thought it was time for his father to be at the station. He rode Lady back across the prairie. At Owl Creek he stopped. He tied Lady to a tree and went toward the house on foot. He wanted to be sure the men from the Black ranch were not there.

In front of the house he saw a man on a horse. At first he thought it was his father. Then he saw other horses and riders. The men from the Black ranch had come, and they were still here!

He hid in the bushes. He heard the men talking.

"I tell you, the horses are gone."

"That boy got away with them. I wish I had my hands on him."

"Let's see what's in here."

The men went into the house.

Dick heard one of them say, "Why don't you light the lamp?"

The door was open. He could see inside the house. A man tried to light the lamp and it fell off the table.

"The house is on fire!" someone said.

"Let it burn!" said another man.

They ran outside.

Dick would have liked to fight the men and drive them away. He would have liked to put out the fire. But he could not drive the men away, and he could not put out the fire by himself.

All he could do was wait.

The men rode around the house and watched it burn. There were five of them. In the light of the fire their faces looked dark and red. One of them had a thin face and a long nose.

"Let's get on down the trail," he said.

"Yes," said another man. "It's nearly time."

They rode away.

Dick came out of the bushes. The roof of the house was burning now. The fire was so hot he could not go near it.

He went down the road to the stable and watched the moon rise. He wished his father would come.

From a long way off he heard the sound of a horse's hoofs. A rider was coming up the trail. Dick kept out of sight. It might be a man from the Black ranch.

The rider came past the stable. He stopped in the light of the burning house.

"*Dick!*" he called.

"Father!" Dick went running to him. "Here I am."

"Dick, what happened? Are you all right?"

"Yes, and so are the horses and the cow." Dick told him what had happened and why the Kellys had gone away.

"If those men had found you," said his father, "I might never have seen you again."

"I saw all the men," said Dick. "There were five of them."

"I know. I saw them, too. They were waiting for me down the trail. They tried to take my horse and the mail."

"They didn't get the mail, did they?"

"No. My horse was faster. I got away."

"George Gates said you would have to take the mail on to the next station. I have another horse here for you, Father. I have Lady tied over there out of sight."

"Good! Bring her here." Mr. Park slid off his horse.

"Your arm is bleeding!" cried Dick.

"Yes. Those men . . . they shot me." Mr. Park's knees bent. He fell at Dick's feet.

XIII

THE WOLF PACK

The horse jumped to one side. Dick caught the bridle reins.

Mr. Park tried to sit up. "Don't let the horse get away. He has the mail on his saddle."

Dick took out his handkerchief. "Can we tie up your arm with this?"

"My arm can wait. The mail has to go through."

Mr. Park got to his feet. His arm hung at his side.

"Father, you can't go on," said Dick.

"I've *got* to go on." Mr. Park started to climb into the saddle and stopped. "I'm so weak. I didn't know I had lost so much blood."

"I'll help you to the stable," said Dick. "You can have a bed on the hay."

"But the mail . . ."

"I'll carry the mail," said Dick.

"Oh, no. It's a long way. You've never been over the trail." Mr. Park looked at Dick. "Do you think you could do it?"

"I know I could," said Dick.

"Something might happen to you."

"Nothing will happen to me. I'll ride Lady, and I can follow the trail."

Mr. Park tried again to get into the saddle, but he was too weak. "Dick, I'm going to let you go," he said. "It's the only way."

Dick took the saddle and the mail off his father's horse and put them on Lady.

"Get there as fast as you can," said Mr. Park.

"I will," said Dick.

He helped his father to the stable. Then he rode away.

The moon was bright. He could see the trail a long way ahead.

"You know this road, don't you, Lady?" he said. "We'll get there, all right."

While he rode, he thought of many things. He thought of the people who were waiting for the mail. "The Pony Express is a chain reaching across the country and holding it together," his father had said. Now, for the first time, Dick felt that he was part of the chain. He wasn't too young to help. Tonight he had saved the horses at Owl Creek Station. Now he was carrying the mail!

He looked back. He was miles from the burning house, but he could still see the light of the fire. He could see something else. A shadow was moving along the trail.

It was too small to be a horse and rider. Dick looked again. This time there were two shadows. They were coming closer.

Lady seemed to know that something was wrong. She shook her head. She laid back her ears.

The next time Dick looked there were more shadows. They looked like big dogs moving together, and they made no sound. All at once Dick knew. The shadows were wolves.

He felt cold, and his mouth was dry. He had never liked to hear the wolves howl at night. Now he was riding with a pack of them at his heels.

If the wolves were hungry enough they might run at Lady's side and drag her down. Or Lady might fall and throw him off in the trail.

He held tight to the saddle. His hand touched a leather pocket. He felt something hard inside. His father's pistol!

He pulled it out. He was careful not to drop it.

He turned in the saddle and pointed the pistol at the nearest wolf. He fired.

The wolf jumped high into the air and fell. The other wolves sprang upon it. Dick heard them howling and fighting.

There was a creek ahead. It was nearly as wide

as a river. Dick looked up and down for a bridge. There was none.

Lady walked into the creek. She went deeper and deeper. The water came higher than Dick's knees. He knew the mail would keep dry. It had oiled silk around it. But he was afraid his father's pistol would get wet. He held it high above his head.

Lady was swimming. Her mane and tail floated out on the water.

"Come on, girl," said Dick.

They were out of the water now. Lady climbed the bank.

Dick looked back. There were no wolves in sight, but he kept the pistol in his hand.

A cloud came over the moon. The night grew dark, and it was hard for Dick to see the trail.

He saw something move ahead. He pulled Lady into some bushes and stopped. A horse and rider came down the trail. A man called out, "Hello!"

Dick thought he and Lady were out of sight, but the man saw them.

"You in the bushes. Is that you, George Gates?"

"Who are you?" asked Dick.

"I'm Frank Martin from Sand Hill Station. The Pony Express is late. I'm looking for the rider."

"I'm the rider," said Dick.

"You?"

"Yes. I'm Dick Park. Some men from Black's ranch burned our house and shot my father, and I had to bring the mail."

"Come with me," said Mr. Martin. "Quick!"

Side by side they rode up the trail. They came to the big log house that was Sand Hill Station.

"Here's my son with another horse." Mr. Martin spoke to the man waiting in the trail. "Take the mail, Joe."

"Yes, sir." Joe took the mail and rode away.

Mr. Martin took Dick into the station. Dick told him all that had happened. "Now I have to go back," he said. "I have to help take care of my father."

"No. I'll ride back and take care of him," said Mr. Martin. "It's time you and your horse had some rest. You can sleep in Joe's bed. When you get up, my wife will get you something to eat."

It was daylight when Dick went into Joe's room. A bed had never looked so good to him before.

ALL'S WELL ALONG THE ROAD

All's well a - long the road,

So the rid-ers say. Good news a-

long the road, All's well to - day.

XIV

"ALL'S WELL ALONG THE ROAD"

Dick slept all day. When he woke up, it was night.

"Stay here till morning," said Mrs. Martin. "Then you won't have to ride in the dark."

So Dick spent the night at Sand Hill Station. Early in the morning he was on the trail again, riding Lady home.

It was still morning when he rode up to Owl Creek Station. He heard someone say, "Here comes

Dick!" The stable door opened and out came Katy. Behind her came Mr. and Mrs. Kelly.

"Where's Father?" asked Dick.

"Here," said Katy.

He saw his father inside the stable. He jumped off his horse and ran to him.

"Are you all right, Dick?" asked Mr. Park.

"Yes, and Lady is, too. Is your arm better?"

"Yes. Mr. Martin took good care of me."

"We are better, too," said Katy, "but Father and I were sick all the way to the doctor's."

"And *I* was sick when we got back and found our house burned," said Mrs. Kelly. "Now I see it could have been ever so much worse."

"Dick, I don't know how to thank you for saving our horses and the cow." Mr. Kelly held out his hand. "Will you shake hands with me and forget what a cross old bear I've been?"

Dick shook hands with him.

Katy said, "Oh, I wish I could have seen you riding with the mail."

"Come on back here and tell me all about it, Son."

Mr. Park led the way to the back of the stable. He opened a window and warm sunlight came in. He and Dick sat on the hay. "A stable may not be so good to live in, but we have a roof over us. Some men are coming in a few days to build a new house."

"Maybe I can help," said Dick.

"You won't be here," said his father.

"Why not?"

"I'm going to take you away."

"Where?" asked Dick.

"Back East. To New York, if you want to go."

"But . . . but why?"

"You never liked it here," said Mr. Park. "I made you stay because I thought it was better for us both. Now I know it wasn't right to keep you here. With men burning houses and trying to steal horses and rob the mail, it's not a safe place for you."

"I'm used to it now," said Dick. "You said it would be better when I got used to it, and it is."

"Don't you want to go back East?" asked his father.

"No. Mr. Kelly needs me to help with the

horses. I never felt like part of the Pony Express until I was out there carrying the mail, and then . . . well . . . now I can see how you feel about it."

"And you want to go on being part of the Pony Express?"

"Yes," said Dick. "That's what I want."

"Son, I'm glad to hear you say that," said Mr. Park. "I'm *glad!*"

George Gates rode up to the stable. He looked in at Dick and his father. The window was so high they could see only his head as he sat on his horse.

"Hello, George," said Mr. Park. "How is everything this morning?"

"All's well along the road," said George. "I've just been to a party."

"A party?" said Mr. Park.

"Mr. Martin and I got some men together, and we all went over to the Black ranch. At first old Billy Black and his boys wanted to play rough. But it wasn't long till they didn't feel like playing any more. We drove them off down the river. They won't be back here again."

"But Little Bear is a good Indian," said Dick. "He came all the way here to tell me the men were coming. He told me to hide so I wouldn't get hurt. You didn't drive him away, did you?"

"No, we didn't drive him away. Look." George held someone up to the window. It was Little Bear. He had been sitting on George's horse.

The Indian boy climbed through the window.

"The men left him behind," said George. "We found him hiding in the barn. He told us he wanted to come here, and Mr. Kelly says he can stay."

George rode away to water his horse. The Indian boy sat down. He looked tired and hungry, but happy.

"Me stay," he said.

"I'm glad you're going to stay," said Dick. "We can ride and hunt and fish together."

"Yes," said Mr. Park. "We want Little Bear to stay. And when we go away, maybe Little Bear can go with us."

"Aren't we going to stay here," asked Dick, "so you can keep riding for the Pony Express when your arm is well?"

"Yes, as long as the Pony Express wants me," said his father. "But some day there will be telegraph lines and railroads all over the West."

"And the country won't need the Pony Express any more?" said Dick.

"No. But people will never forget the Pony Express and all it did to hold the East and West together," said Mr. Park. "Some day we will see roads and farms and cities all the way from here to California, and the country will thank the Pony Express for helping build up the West and make it a great place to live."

"You go California, me go, too," said Little Bear.

"I don't know yet about California," said Mr. Park. "I'll tell you what I want to do. I want to go back to St. Joe and find my friend Sam Harper. Then we'll all go West and find a little valley with mountains and pine trees all around it. We'll build a cabin there, and that will be our home."

"Me like," said Little Bear.

"I'll like it, too," said Dick.

They sat there a long time, looking into the sunshine.

"Don't you boys want to lie down and rest?" asked Mr. Park. "Aren't you sleepy?"

"No," said Dick, and Little Bear shook his head. They were both wide awake as they sat with their faces turned toward the West that would some day be their home.